Whispers Beneath The Tides

A Novel of Love, Secrets, and Second Chances

Trevor Jensen

Dedication

For anyone who's ever returned to a place they swore they'd left behind—
and for the heart that still remembers why it mattered.

To those who have loved deeply, lost silently, and found their way back to something braver.

And to every reader who believes some tides never stop pulling you home.
This story is for you.

—TJ

Introduction

In Salt Haven, the past is never truly past. It breathes in the salt spray, echoes in the cry of the gulls, and hides in the cold, dark spaces beneath the pier. The ocean keeps the town's secrets, pulling them under with the tide, only to whisper them back to shore when you least expect it.

Every summer, the town swells with the hopeful and the heartbroken, those looking to lose themselves in the sun and sand. But for the ones who call it home, returning is a more complicated affair. It's a reckoning with the ghosts you thought you'd outrun, a confrontation with the person you used to be.

This is the story of a summer when a girl who had lost her voice and a boy who had lost his way were pulled into the same orbit. She was haunted by a secret she couldn't remember; he was anchored by a tragedy he couldn't forget. Drawn together by sleepless nights and sorrows too heavy to carry alone, they discovered that healing sometimes means risking a broken heart all over again.

They sought solace in the quiet spaces between the waves, but in a town built on whispers, some secrets refuse to stay buried. When the tide pulls back, it reveals everything that's been hiding in the deep: heartbreak, hope, and the terrifying, beautiful promise of a second chance.

Dedication

For those who walk alone through the storm.

To the ones who've stared down the dark and kept going.To the ones who ask the hard questions when the answers cost too much.To those who carry ghosts not because they want to—but because someone has to.

This story is for the broken, the relentless, the quietly brave.May you always find your way, even when the rain never stops.

— C.B.

Contents

Chapter 1: Salt Air, Old Wounds

The storm that welcomed Mandy Kline home to Salt Haven was not on any forecast. It was a personal, vindictive squall, born of the same moody stretch of Atlantic that had shaped her childhood. One minute, the late June sun was melting over the horizon, painting the boardwalk in hues of apricot and rose. The next, the sky bruised to a violent purple, and the ocean, that great, indifferent beast, roared to life.

The wind hit first, a physical blow that stole the air from her lungs and whipped her wild curly hair across her face. It carried the scent of ozone, of salt, and of something else she couldn't name—the smell of a place that no longer recognized her. Rain followed, not in gentle drops but in hard, cold sheets that plastered her thin sundress to her skin in seconds. She tasted it on her lips, briny and sharp, a baptism she hadn't asked for.

Clutching the strap of her worn leather satchel, Mandy ducked under the awning of "The Salty Scoop," its cheerful, hand-painted sign a mockery of the tempest. The ice cream shop was closed, its windows dark. Everything felt closed. She had been home for exactly four hours, and the sense of alienation was already a physical weight in her chest, a cold, hard stone of dread.

This was supposed to be her sanctuary. After a brutal first year at college, a year that had systematically dismantled her confidence and left her feeling like a ghost haunting her own life, Salt Haven was meant to be the cure. She had pictured long, quiet days spent with her toes in the sand, the familiar rhythm of the tides slowly piecing her back together. She had not pictured this: a furious, unwelcoming sky and a hollow ache that the familiar sights only seemed to amplify.

The town looked the same, yet different, like a photograph of a memory she could no longer quite feel. The arcade still blinked its gaudy promises into the growing dark. A woman pushing a stroller offered a thin, polite smile as she hurried past. Mandy recognized her—Sarah-Jane from her chemistry class. For a split second, Mandy wasn't on the rainy boardwalk; she was back in the harsh fluorescent light of the school cafeteria, hearing the snickering, the whispered word—*freak*—that had followed her for months. The memory was so sharp it made her flinch, pulling her secondhand cardigan tighter as if it were armor. They remembered Mandy Kline, the quiet girl who always had a book. They did not know this new version, the one who felt brittle as sea glass, one wrong step away from shattering.

A figure emerged from the swirling mist, a woman walking with a steady, unhurried pace, her bright yellow raincoat a beacon in the gloom. It was Mrs. Leona Brooks, the town's retired librarian, her silver hair escaping her hood in a wispy halo. She moved with the serene purpose of someone who understood storms, both literal and metaphorical.

"Well now," Mrs. Brooks said, her voice a low, melodic hum that cut through the wind's shriek. She stopped beside Mandy, her gaze, as sharp and clear as a winter morning, taking in Mandy's soaked dress and the tremor in her hands. "The ocean seems to have a lot to say this evening."

Mandy managed a tight, watery smile. "It's not saying anything very friendly."

"It rarely does to those who have forgotten its language," Mrs. Brooks replied, a cryptic warmth in her eyes. She didn't ask what Mandy was doing here, or why she looked like a drowned kitten. Mrs. Brooks had a way of seeing past the surface of things, of addressing the wound without needing to poke at it. "Sometimes, the best thing to do when the world is shouting is to find the quietest room you can and listen to what your own heart has to say in response."

The words settled over Mandy, a strange comfort. In a town where she felt scrutinized, Mrs. Brooks's observation felt like a blanket. "I'm not sure I'd like what it has to say."

"Perhaps not," the old woman conceded, her eyes crinkling at the corners. "But it's speaking whether you listen or not. Better to know the words." She gave Mandy's arm a gentle squeeze, her touch surprisingly firm. "The library is dry. And the kettle is always on."

With a final, knowing nod, Mrs. Brooks continued her walk, disappearing back into the rain as mysteriously as she had appeared. Mandy watched her go, the librarian's words echoing in her mind. *Listen to what your own heart has to say.* Her heart was just a frantic, terrified bird, beating its wings against the cage of her ribs.

The storm began to relent, its fury softening to a steady, percussive drumming on the awning. Across the street, the lights of a pickup truck cut through the deepening twilight, its engine rumbling to a stop near the pier. A figure climbed out, and even from this distance, silhouetted against the churning waves, Mandy knew who it was.

Logan Reyes.

He was a landmark in Salt Haven, as fixed and elemental as the lighthouse at the point. Or he had been. The boy she remembered was golden, his laughter as easy and bright as the summer sun. He had been the star quarterback, the effortless charmer, the one who moved through their small town with an uncomplicated grace that everyone envied.

The man standing there now was a stranger.

His shoulders were broader, but they were hunched against more than the rain. He moved with a heavy, deliberate slowness, his head down. The easy grace was gone, replaced by a coiled tension that was visible even from fifty yards away. He walked to the edge of the pier, his hands shoved deep into the pockets of his jacket, and just stood there, a solitary figure staring into the violent churn of the sea.

Everyone knew what had happened. They knew about the accident, about his brother, about the scholarship he'd lost. The whispers had followed him for a year, a corrosive tide of gossip and pity. Seeing him now, Mandy felt a painful lurch of recognition. He was a different kind of ghost than she was, but he was a ghost all the same. Haunted. She watched him, and noticed his right hand, at his side, clenching and unclenching in a rhythmic, nervous gesture. She looked down at her own hand, realizing with a jolt that her fingers were doing the exact same thing, squeezing the worn strap of her satchel in a desperate, repeating pattern. He was a storm of his own, and she knew, with a certainty that chilled her more than the rain, that she needed to stay far, far away from that kind of wreckage.

Finally turning away, she began the walk home, her sneakers squelching with every step. The air was thick with the post-storm smell of wet asphalt and damp earth. Home was a small, salt-bleached cottage three blocks from the beach, a place that held the scent of her mother's lavender soap and her father's pipe tobacco. It should have been the safest place in the world.

Inside, she dripped her way up to her childhood bedroom. It was exactly as she'd left it, a time capsule of a girl she no longer was. The walls were covered in posters of bands she didn't listen to anymore. The shelves were crammed with books she had read a dozen times, their spines soft and yielding. Her gaze fell on a stack of journals on her nightstand, their covers faded and worn.

She picked up the top one, its navy blue cover warped from some long-forgotten spill. This was the journal from her senior year of high school, the year before everything had fallen apart. Her fingers, still numb with cold, fumbled with the pages. She had intended to find a blank page, to pour out the misery of the day, to try and make sense of the tangled knot of emotions inside her.

But the journal fell open to the very last entry. Tucked into the spine of the book, a single, dried beach pea petal—its purple color faded to a ghostly lavender—fluttered out and landed on her bedspread. Her breath caught. She hadn't seen one of those since senior year, since that night at the dunes. Then her eyes fell on the words on the page, and the blood turned to ice in her veins.

The handwriting was hers, but it was frantic, slanted, the ink slightly smeared as if by tears. It was a single, cryptic line.

He knows. He saw everything. Don't let him tell.

Mandy stared at the words, her hand hovering over the fragile petal. The storm outside was nothing compared to the one that had just broken inside her. The rain-soaked chill she'd felt on the boardwalk was suddenly a deep, penetrating cold that had nothing to do with the weather. She sank onto the edge of her bed, the journal clutched in her hand.

She had no memory of writing this. No idea who "he" was. But as she stared at the petal, a dark, forgotten door in the back of her mind creaked open, and the faint, terrifying whisper of a memory she had buried long ago began to stir. This summer wasn't going to be about healing. It was going to be about survival.

Chapter 2: Driftwood Fires

Sleep offered no escape. Mandy's dreams were a tangled mess of churning gray waves and a single, ghostly lavender petal that pulsed with a malevolent light. She kept hearing a whisper, a venomous word she couldn't quite catch, just on the edge of her hearing. She woke with a gasp, the cryptic words from her journal—*He knows. He saw everything*—seared onto the back of her eyelids. The sun was streaming through her window, a cheerful, golden liar. Her fear hadn't vanished with the night; it had simply settled, a cold, heavy sediment in the pit of her stomach.

Her phone buzzed on the nightstand. It was a text from Tessa Gilroy.

BEACH BONFIRE. TONIGHT. 8 PM. SANDY POINT. NO EXCUSES. I'M DRAGGING YOU OUT OF THE HOUSE IF I HAVE TO. <3

Mandy's first instinct was to curl into a ball and refuse. The thought of facing a crowd, of navigating the treacherous currents of small talk when she felt so raw, was exhausting. But Tessa was a force of nature, a cheerful hurricane of loyalty that Mandy had never been able to resist. Besides, hiding in her room would only give the ghosts more space to crowd in.

That evening, as dusk bled across the sky, Mandy found her way to Sandy Point. A massive bonfire was already blazing, a roaring beast of orange and gold that spat embers into the twilight. The smell of burning driftwood, sharp and clean, mingled with the salty air. A circle of familiar faces was gathered around its warmth.

"You came!" Tessa detached herself from the group and threw her arms around Mandy in a fierce hug that smelled of coconut sunscreen and home. "I was about to send a search party."

"You would have," Mandy murmured into her friend's shoulder, a genuine smile touching her lips for the first time all day.

"Damn right, I would have," Tessa said, pulling back, her eyes scanning Mandy's face with concern. "You look... pale. College drain all the life out of you?"

"Something like that," Mandy said, the understatement hanging between them.

Tessa, ever perceptive, let it go. "Well, you're here now. Come on, say hi." She tugged Mandy toward the fire. "You know Jonah."

Jonah Mercer, his face split in a wide, easy grin, waved a half-eaten s'more at her. "Kline! Welcome back to the land of the living."

"Trying to, anyway," Mandy replied, feeling a bit of her tension ease.

"And this is Caleb," Tessa said, her voice a little tighter.

Caleb Munroe didn't smile. He gave a curt nod, his eyes, dark and assessing, lingering on Mandy for a moment too long. A cold dread trickled down her spine as he looked at her. His face was familiar from the hallways of high school, a face she associated with the periphery of Logan's golden circle. Could it be him? Was he the 'he' from the journal? The thought was a jolt of ice water, making her skin prickle with a new, more specific fear. Where Logan's grief had made him withdraw, it seemed to have sharpened Caleb's edges, leaving him bitter and serrated. He was a storm cloud in their cheerful circle.

They settled onto a large piece of driftwood, Mandy trying to ignore the sudden, frantic thumping of her heart. She watched the flames dance, mesmerized by the way they consumed the wood, turning solid memories into ash and smoke.

That's when Logan arrived.

He materialized at the edge of the firelight, a shadow detaching itself from the deeper darkness of the dunes. The easy chatter around the fire faltered.

Caleb didn't just harden his jaw. He muttered, just loud enough for those nearby to hear, "Look what the tide dragged in."

The remark was so sharp, so full of venom, that it made the air feel thin.

Logan's eyes, flat and cold, flickered to him. "Still here, Caleb?" he said, his voice devoid of emotion. "I'm surprised."

The exchange was brutal, a flash of lightning that illuminated the chasm of wreckage between them. Logan's gaze slid away from Caleb's, sweeping over the group before it landed, for a brief, shocking second, on Mandy. It wasn't a look of recognition, not really. It was something deeper, a flicker of shared understanding, as if he saw the same fractured quality in her that he felt in himself. The air crackled. She felt an inexplicable pull toward his quiet, wounded stillness, a dangerous curiosity that defied all her instincts.

He gave a barely perceptible nod to the group and then moved to the far side of the fire, putting as much distance as he could between himself and Caleb. He sat on the sand, his back against a dune, effectively outside their circle. The invisible wall around him was so palpable it was almost shimmering.

The conversation eventually stuttered back to life, but the energy had shifted. Logan's silent, brooding presence changed the very chemistry of the night. Mandy found herself acutely aware of him, of the way he stared into the fire as if searching for an answer in the flames.

Tessa, sensing Mandy's distraction, leaned in close. "Don't," she whispered, her voice low and firm.

Mandy blinked, turning to her friend. "Don't what?"

"Don't try to fix him," Tessa said, her expression serious. "He's a mess, Mandy. Has been ever since his brother... and after what happened with Jenna last summer... He just breaks things now. Even when he doesn't mean to."

Jenna. Mandy remembered her. A cheerleader from the year above them. The name added a new layer to the story, a history of wreckage that made the warning feel less like advice and more like a prophecy. Still, Mandy's empathy was a reflex. She saw a kindred spirit in Logan's isolation, a reflection of her own guarded heart. She felt the pull, gravitational and terrifying.

An hour later, lulled by the fire's warmth, Mandy found herself listening to Jonah talk about the summer programs.

"...and the town cut the library's budget again, can you believe it?" he was saying. "Mrs. Brooks is trying to keep the children's reading program going on her own, but she needs volunteers. No one's signing up."

The words sliced through Mandy's anxious fog. The library. Mrs. Brooks. A quiet room full of books and stories. It was a lifeline.

Before she could second-guess herself, the words were tumbling out of her mouth.

"I'll do it," Mandy said.

The conversation stopped. Everyone turned to look at her. Tessa's eyes were wide with surprise. Jonah's face broke into a massive grin. Caleb glanced over, a flicker of something unreadable in his expression.

"Seriously?" Jonah asked.

"Yes," Mandy said, her voice gaining strength. "I can volunteer. I'd like to."

The decision felt like a key turning in a lock. It was a step toward something, instead of a retreat away from everything. For the first time since she'd arrived home, a tiny, fragile shoot of purpose began to unfurl within her.

From across the fire, in the deep shadows by the dunes, she saw Logan lift his head. His eyes met hers again, and this time, the look was different. The weary mask had slipped, and for a fleeting moment, she saw a flicker of raw, unguarded surprise. And something else. Something that looked almost like hope.

The connection was brief, a spark that lived and died in a heartbeat, but it was enough. It was enough to make her heart skip, enough to make her forget, for one precious second, the cryptic warning tucked away in her bedroom and the terrifying possibility that the source of her fear was sitting just a few feet away. The bonfire crackled, sending a shower of golden embers into the star-dusted sky, and Mandy felt the first, tentative whisper of a new beginning.

Chapter 3: Dog-Eared Beginnings

The Salt Haven Public Library was the one place in town that felt like a true sanctuary. It smelled of old paper, lemon polish, and quiet contemplation. The morning after the bonfire, Mandy pushed open the heavy oak door and felt a sense of peace settle over her for the first time since her return. Her decision from the night before, made in a moment of bonfire-fueled bravery, felt solid and right in the light of day.

Mrs. Brooks was waiting for her behind the circulation desk. "Ah, the volunteer arrives," she said, her smile warm. "I had a feeling the books were calling to you."

"They were shouting, actually," Mandy admitted.

"They tend to do that when a soul is in need of a story." Mrs. Brooks handed her a canvas bag filled with picture books. "The reading circle is in the children's wing. They're a little shy at first, but they're good listeners."

Mandy's first session was a clumsy, nerve-wracking dance. Her voice felt thin, her hands trembled, and the familiar, cold tendrils of self-doubt began to creep in. *You can't even do this right.*

She was struggling through a page when the bell above the library door chimed. A moment later, Logan Reyes appeared in the archway of the children's wing.

Her heart hammered against her ribs for two reasons at once. The first was simple, terrifying social math: he was Logan Reyes, broken and beautiful and entirely off-limits. The second was a colder, more primal fear. As he stood silhouetted in the archway, her mind flashed to the note—*He knows.* The thought was absurd, she told herself, squashing it instantly. But it left a residue of ice in her veins.

In the bright, gentle light of the library, he just looked... tired. He was holding the hand of a small, dark-haired girl with his same deep brown eyes, who was hiding shyly behind his leg. His gaze met Mandy's, and he froze.

"Sorry," Logan mumbled, his voice a low rumble that felt too large for the quiet space. "Didn't mean to interrupt."

The little girl, however, seemed to have caught a thread of the story, her eyes fixed on the picture of the grumpy badger. "Is he mad?" she whispered.

Mandy's heart gave a little lurch. "He is," she said softly. "He thinks he wants to be alone, but I think he's just lonely."

The girl, Ella, took a hesitant step forward. "Why is he lonely?"

"Ella, we're bothering them," Logan said, his tone gruff but his touch gentle.

"No, you're not," Mandy said quickly. "It's a good question."

Mrs. Brooks chose that moment to glide into the wing. "Logan Reyes. And Ella. What a treat." She smiled at the little girl. "I have a book here about a star that was afraid of the dark. Do you think a star could be afraid of the dark?"

Ella giggled. "That's silly. The dark is where they live."

"Exactly," Mrs. Brooks said, her wise eyes flicking between them all. "Sometimes we're most afraid of the very things we're meant to live in."

The moment was broken. Logan cleared his throat, steering Ella toward a row of shelves. Mandy finished the story, her voice a little steadier, but she was intensely aware of him. When the session was over, she began gathering the books.

As she reached for the last one, the book about the grumpy badger slipped from her trembling fingers. She bent to retrieve it at the exact same moment Logan moved to help.

Their hands brushed.

It was a brief, electric shock of contact that made her snatch her hand back as if burned. His eyes met hers, wide with surprise, and for a second, the air was thick with something new, something that had nothing to do with grief or little sisters. He was close enough now that she could smell the faint, clean scent of salt and soap clinging to his t-shirt. It was a simple, grounding smell that felt completely at odds with the storm of gossip that surrounded him.

"She liked the story," he said, his voice suddenly husky. He cleared his throat and took a step back, breaking the spell. Ella was clutching a stack of books, her face buried in his side.

"She's a good listener," Mandy replied, her heart thudding a chaotic rhythm against her ribs.

An awkward silence fell, charged with the ghost of their touch.

"Look," he said suddenly, running a hand through his short, dark hair. "My mom's working double shifts at the diner all summer. And with... everything... Ella's been quiet. She won't talk to anyone." He looked down at his sister with a fierce, aching tenderness that made Mandy's breath catch. "But she talked to you."

His gaze lifted to meet hers, raw and vulnerable. "I have to work at the beach in the afternoons. I was wondering... if it's not too much trouble... could you maybe... keep an eye on her? After school? Just for an hour or so, until I can pick her up."

The request hung in the air, a fragile bridge built over the crackling space their brief touch had created. It was a plea for help, an act of trust. Tessa's warning echoed in her mind. *He just breaks things now.* But looking at the desperation in his eyes, Mandy knew she couldn't say no.

"Okay," she heard herself say, her voice soft but clear. "Yes. Of course."

A wave of relief washed over Logan's face, so profound it was like watching the sun break through the clouds. "Really? Thank you." The words were simple, but they carried an immense weight. "I'll... I owe you one."

He and Ella checked out their books. As they were leaving, Ella turned and gave Mandy a small, shy wave. Mandy waved back, a real, unforced smile reaching her eyes.

She stood alone in the quiet of the children's wing, the scent of old books all around her. Her heart was a confused, fluttering thing. She had just tied herself to Logan

Reyes, the one person she knew she should avoid. It was a mistake. It was dangerous. But as she re-shelved the book about the grumpy badger, her fingers still tingling from where his hand had brushed hers, she couldn't shake the feeling that it was the first right decision she had made all summer.

Chapter 4: Rip Currents

The next few days settled into a fragile rhythm. In the mornings, Mandy would volunteer at the library. In the afternoons, Ella would appear, a silent, book-clutching shadow who would read until Logan, smelling of salt and sun, would arrive to pick her up. Their exchanges were brief, awkward orbits around the circulation desk, the memory of their brushed hands a constant, humming presence between them. Mandy found herself listening for the chime of the library door around four o'clock, her heart giving a ridiculous little leap when she saw his familiar silhouette.

Late that afternoon, Mandy took her journal and walked to the boardwalk. She found an empty bench at the far end of the pier, the sun beginning its slow, fiery descent.

As she opened her journal, her thoughts kept snagging on that single, terrifying line: *He knows. He saw everything.*

Her head snapped up as a pair of girls from her high school class ambled past. One of them, a blonde named Becca who had always been at the center of the clique that tormented her, met Mandy's eyes. A slow, knowing smirk spread across Becca's face. She leaned in and whispered something to her friend, who glanced back at Mandy and giggled. The sound was like a physical blow, instantly transporting Mandy back to the harsh fluorescent lights of the school cafeteria, to the crushing weight of her own inadequacy. The poison of the past was still potent, turning her sanctuary into a place of threats.

A shadow fell over her page. "Mind if I...?"

Mandy jumped, slamming her journal shut. Logan was standing there, dressed in running shorts and a faded t-shirt, his chest still heaving slightly from a jog.

"No, of course not," she stammered.

He sat, leaving a careful distance between them. They sat in silence for a long moment, two solitary people sharing a single, vast view.

"It's a rip current out there today," he said finally, his voice quiet. He leaned in closer to point, and his arm brushed against hers. The contact was brief, but it sent a jolt of warmth through her. "You see how the surface looks calm in that one spot? That's how it tricks you. It looks like a safe place, a way out. But underneath, it's pulling everything out to sea."

Mandy, hyper-aware of his closeness, followed his gaze. "I never knew that."

"Most people don't," he said, a bitter edge to his voice. He leaned back, but the space between them now felt charged. "They only see the surface." He finally turned to look at her, his eyes dark with a pain that went far beyond the tide. "The ocean... it doesn't forget. It holds onto everything. Every mistake, every regret. It just pulls it under and keeps it down there in the cold."

His words were a confession. He was talking about his brother. Mandy's heart ached for him. Instead of a platitude, she offered a piece of her own truth. "There's a poem," she said softly. "By Rilke. It says, 'Let everything happen to you: beauty and terror. Just keep going. No feeling is final.'"

Logan was quiet for a long time. He was watching her, his expression intense, as if seeing her for the first time. His eyes dropped to her lips for a fraction of a second before meeting her gaze again. "'No feeling is final,'" he repeated, the words tasting strange and hopeful in his mouth. "I like that."

The moment was shattered by the buzz of Mandy's phone. A text from Tessa: *Storm warning. Big one's rolling in tonight. Get home safe!*

A low rumble of thunder echoed from far out at sea. The sky to the east was darkening at an unnatural speed.

"You should go," Logan said, standing up, the brief connection broken. "It's going to be bad."

He started to jog away, then stopped abruptly. Mandy followed his gaze and saw it: Caleb's mud-splattered truck, parked across the street near the diner. Logan's jaw tightened for a moment, a flicker of anger in his eyes, before he turned back to her.

"Thanks," he said, and the word held a world of meaning. "For the poem."

And then he was gone, a solitary figure disappearing down the boardwalk. Mandy stood, clutching her journal, the wind beginning to whip her hair around her face. The approaching storm felt like a premonition, a physical manifestation of all the unspoken grief and fear—both human and elemental—that swirled around Salt Haven. And she was standing right in the middle of it.

Chapter 5: Gathering Clouds

The wind that chased Mandy off the pier was a wild, frantic thing. It tore at the awnings of the board-walk shops and sent sand skittering across the weathered planks like tiny, panicked creatures. Instead of heading home, a magnetic, inexplicable pull drew her toward the warm, glowing windows of the Salt Haven Diner. The sight of Caleb's truck had planted a seed of dread in her mind, a fear for Logan that momentarily eclipsed her own.

The bell above the diner door jingled. The place was crowded, a noisy, steamy haven from the escalating storm. She saw them immediately, tucked into a booth in the back corner: Tessa and Jonah, their faces etched with concern, and across from them, Logan and Caleb. The tension was a physical force.

Tessa caught Mandy's eye and gave a tiny, desperate shake of her head, a clear warning: *Stay away.*

But Mandy couldn't. She slid into the booth next to Tessa, her heart hammering.

Jonah's face flooded with relief. "Mandy! Just the person we need. Tell these two idiots to stop trying to stare holes in the table."

"There's nothing to talk about," Caleb snapped, his dark eyes flicking to Mandy with annoyance before settling back on Logan. "Some of us have things to do. Others just like to sit around feeling sorry for themselves."

"Caleb, stop it," Tessa warned.

"What?" Caleb shot back. "It's true. Saint Logan, the town tragedy. Can't even be bothered to help his old friends with the one thing he was ever good at."

Logan's head snapped toward him, his eyes blazing. "You want my help? After everything? You've got a hell of a nerve."

"I've got a regatta to win," Caleb retorted. "Something you might remember caring about, before you decided to give up on everything. And everyone." The last two words were aimed like poisoned darts. A flicker of profound, gut-wrenching pain crossed Logan's face.

Mandy felt a surge of protective anger. "That's not fair," she said, her voice trembling but clear. "You don't know what he's going through."

Caleb let out a short, bitter laugh. "Oh, I don't? I was there, sweetheart. I saw the whole thing."

The words slammed into Mandy with the force of a physical blow. The air left her lungs. The noisy diner faded to a dull roar in her ears, and for a terrifying second, the only thing she could see was the frantic, tear-smeared handwriting in her journal. It wasn't just a memory anymore. It was a threat, sitting right across the table from her.

"Shut up, Caleb," Logan said, his voice dangerously low.

Before he could move, Tessa reached across the table and put a hand on Caleb's arm. "That's enough," she said, her voice low and fierce. "Whatever this is, you're done."

Caleb just shook her off, his eyes still locked on Logan with a look of pure venom.

With a finality that felt like a door slamming shut, Logan pushed himself out of the booth. "I'm done." He threw a few crumpled bills onto the table and stalked toward the door. The storm outside broke in earnest, the rain now a torrential downpour.

"I should go after him," Mandy said, starting to slide out of the booth.

"No, Mandy, don't," Tessa pleaded, grabbing her arm. "He needs to cool off. You'll just get caught in the cross-fire."

But Mandy saw the look on Logan's face as he shoved the diner door open—it wasn't just anger. It was a deep, bottomless despair. The look of a man being pulled under.

She ignored Tessa's plea and followed him out into the raging storm. "Logan, wait!" she shouted.

He was already halfway across the street. At the same time, Caleb burst out of the diner behind her.

"Logan, you coward!" Caleb bellowed, his voice raw with a year's worth of unprocessed grief and rage. "You can't just walk away!"

Logan stopped and turned, his face a mask of fury. "I told you to leave it alone, Caleb!"

They stood there, two former best friends, ready to tear each other apart while the sky fell down around them.

Suddenly, a high, panicked scream cut through the noise of the storm. It came from the direction of the beach. "Help! Somebody, help me! My little boy! He's only ten years old!"

The words struck the air like lightning. Ten. The age Logan's brother had been.

All three of them froze, their personal drama instantly incinerated by the raw terror in that cry. They turned toward the sound, toward the dark, churning chaos of the ocean. A woman was stumbling near the edge of the waves, her voice swallowed by the wind.

"He was just here!" she shrieked. "He's gone!"

Logan didn't hesitate. The anger on his face was replaced by a sharp, focused alarm that was more terrifying than rage. He was running headlong into the ghost of his worst nightmare to prevent it from happening again. He broke into a dead sprint toward the sound, toward the raging water.

"Call 911!" he yelled back at them, his voice already faint against the storm.

Caleb stood frozen for a second, his face pale with a new kind of horror. Then he, too, started running. Mandy stood paralyzed on the wet pavement, her mind reeling. A child was missing. In the water. In this storm.

And Logan, the boy who was haunted by the sea, was running straight into it.

Chapter 6: Stormy Reckonings

The world dissolved into a maelstrom of roaring wind and blinding rain. Mandy's paralysis broke, replaced by a surge of adrenaline so potent it tasted metallic. She fumbled for her phone, her fingers slick and clumsy, and managed to dial 911, her voice a thin shout against the storm's fury as she relayed the horror of a child lost to the waves.

When she looked up, Logan was already a silhouette at the edge of the churning surf. Caleb was right behind him, his earlier animosity burned away by the immediate, primal need to help. Mandy didn't think. She just ran.

"Mandy, no!" Tessa grabbed her arm as she reached the beach. "It's too dangerous!"

But Mandy pulled free. She couldn't be a ghost on the sidelines of this tragedy, too. She ran along the shoreline, her eyes straining to pierce the gloom. Logan and Caleb were working together, moving with the practiced, desperate efficiency of two people who knew the ocean's treachery. The rain was relentless, blurring the world into a terrifying watercolor of gray and black.

But Mandy's eyes, accustomed to searching for details in the quiet gloom of a library, caught it first. A flash of color where there should be none.

"There!" she screamed, her voice raw and torn by the wind, pointing frantically down the beach. "I see him!"

It was a small, bright blue jacket, bobbing in the violent churn. A wave crashed over it, and it was gone.

"I see him!" Logan yelled, and without a moment's hesitation, he dove into an oncoming wave, his powerful lifeguard stroke cutting through the chaos.

Time seemed to warp into an agonizing, breathless eternity. Then, a shout of triumph. Logan had him. He and Caleb stumbled out of the surf, collapsing onto the wet sand. The boy was coughing, sputtering, but he was alive. Paramedics, their lights flashing through the storm, were sprinting down the beach with a gurney.

The immediate crisis was over, but the aftermath was a landscape of raw, fractured emotion. From a distance,

Caleb watched. He stood awkwardly as the paramedics worked, the bitter triumph he'd worn in the diner gone, replaced by a look of pale, horrified understanding. He saw not the rival he'd been baiting, but the broken friend he'd lost a year ago, kneeling in the sand. He took a half-step toward them, then stopped, a man caught in his own rip current of guilt and regret, before turning and melting back into the storm.

Mandy's eyes found Logan. He was on his knees, his head bowed, his body trembling with the aftershocks of a battle he had been forced to fight twice. Without thinking, she went to him. She knelt in the sand beside him and put a hand on his back. He flinched, then seemed to lean into her touch.

"You saved him," she whispered, her voice choked with tears.

He shook his head. "I almost didn't," he rasped. "It was just like..."

He couldn't finish. The grief he had held at bay for a year came rushing in, a tsunami of pain. A ragged sob tore from his throat, a sound of such profound agony that it felt like a physical blow to Mandy's own chest. She could feel the violent tremors running through his entire body under her hand.

She didn't offer words. There were no words for this. Instead, she just stayed there. And then, something shifted. In the midst of the wind and the rain, his hand found hers in the sand. His fingers, numb with cold and trembling, laced with hers. It wasn't a gentle touch; it was a desperate, grasping hold, the grip of a drowning man finding the one solid thing in a world that had dissolved into chaos.

And Mandy, the girl who was terrified of being seen, held on just as tightly, not wanting to ever let go.

Chapter 7: Accidental Confessions

The world outside their small, desperate bubble of contact was a blur of flashing lights and shouting voices. Her entire universe had contracted to the feeling of Logan's trembling hand locked in hers and the raw, ragged sound of his breathing.

"We have to get you out of the rain," she said, her voice low and steady, a strange calm settling over her. "You're freezing."

He didn't seem to hear her. He was still on his knees, staring at the spot on the sand where the boy had lain.

"Logan," she said again, squeezing his hand. "Logan, look at me."

Slowly, he lifted his head. His eyes were unfocused, lost in a private hell. "My truck," he rasped.

With a strength she didn't know she possessed, Mandy helped him to his feet. They reached his old pickup, and she gently took the keys from his shaking hands, unlocking the door and helping him slide in before running around to the passenger side.

Suddenly, they were encased in a startling, profound silence. The roar of the storm was instantly muffled, reduced to a dull drumming on the roof. The only sounds in the cab were their own ragged breaths.

Logan just sat there, shivering uncontrollably. "I saw his face," he whispered, his voice cracking. "When I pulled him from the water. For a second... I thought it was Michael."

The name hung in the air between them. Michael. His brother.

"I couldn't save him," Logan choked out, the words torn from a place of deep, hidden agony. "The undertow was too strong. I had him... I had his hand, and he just... slipped."

The words—*a hand slipping away in the dark*—sent a chill through Mandy that had nothing to do with the cold. A fragmented, terrifying image flashed in her mind: the dunes at night, a panicked cry, the feeling of falling.

She shoved it back down, her heart pounding. This was Logan's story, not hers. But for a terrifying second, it had felt like both.

When his words trailed off into a shuddering silence, she found herself speaking, her own confession an instinctive offering in return. "When I was at college," she began, "I felt like I was invisible. I was so scared of saying the wrong thing, of proving that I didn't belong, that I just... stopped talking."

Logan turned his head slowly, his gaze finally focusing on her. He was truly seeing her. "It felt like drowning," she admitted. "In a quiet, empty room."

He reached out, his cold, trembling fingers closing gently around her wrist. His thumb brushed against her pulse point, a small, intimate gesture that sent a shockwave through her. She could see the flecks of gold in his dark eyes, smell the rain on his skin. The space between them became impossibly small, charged with a year of unspoken grief and a few minutes of terrifying, profound connection.

"You're not invisible," he said, his voice thick with emotion.

The intensity of his gaze was too much, a dangerous current threatening to pull them both under. Just then, Logan's eyes widened with a new alarm. "Ella," he breathed. "Oh God, Ella. She's at home. She's all alone."

The spell was broken. He fumbled for the ignition and started the truck.

"I'll look out for her," Mandy said quickly. "Logan, I mean it. She won't be alone."

He looked at her, his eyes filled with a profound, desperate gratitude. "Thank you," he whispered.

He drove her home, the short ride thick with unspoken emotions. As she got out, she turned back to find him watching her. Before she could lose her nerve, she leaned over and gently squeezed his arm. "No feeling is final," she whispered.

A ghost of a smile touched his lips. She ran through the rain to her front door. As she fumbled for her keys, she heard voices from the porch next door.

"—such a tragedy," Mrs. Gable was saying. "That poor Reyes boy. Always seems to be at the center of it."

"And that Kline girl," Mr. Gable added. "Heard from my nephew who goes to her college that she just... stopped talking. Wouldn't say a word in class. Just sits there like a ghost."

The word *ghost* hit Mandy like a physical slap. She had just confessed her deepest, most specific shame in the sanctuary of his truck, and here it was, bouncing around on a neighbor's porch as casual, cruel gossip. The feeling of being seen evaporated, replaced by the cold, familiar sting of shame. She finally got the door open and slipped inside, the sound of her neighbors' whispers following her, reigniting all her oldest and deepest fears.

Chapter 8: Salt and Storytime

The next morning, the world was washed clean. The storm had passed, leaving behind a sky of impossible, brilliant blue. But Mandy felt none of its renewal. The neighbors' words had been a corrosive acid, eating away at the fragile courage she had found in Logan's truck. She was a ghost again, her shame a heavy shroud.

But she had made a promise.

She forced herself to go to the library. The quiet sanctuary was a balm to her frayed nerves. Just after noon, Ella Reyes slipped into the children's wing, a silent testament to the fragile trust they had built. Mandy's heart ached. Looking at Ella, she knew she couldn't retreat.

Mandy picked up a picture book and sat on the floor near Ella. "Do you want to hear a story?" she asked softly. Ella gave a small, hesitant nod. As Mandy read, she lost herself in the story, and some of the tension in her shoulders began to ease.

"She's missed that," a voice said. Mrs. Brooks was standing in the archway, a gentle smile on her face. "She's missed getting lost in a story." The librarian's eyes were full of a knowing sympathy. "Come with me, dear."

She led Mandy to a small door at the back of the library, unlocking it with an old brass key. "This was the original librarian's office. I call it the secret room." It was small and cozy, with a worn velvet armchair and a window overlooking a tiny garden. "Sometimes," Mrs. Brooks said, placing the key in Mandy's hand, "the main library can feel a bit too... public. When you and Ella need a quieter space, this is yours."

The gesture was so full of understanding that tears pricked Mandy's eyes. "Thank you," she whispered.

"Everyone deserves a place where their story is safe," Mrs. Brooks replied before leaving her alone.

A few moments later, Logan appeared in the doorway. His defenses were gone, his face open and vulnerable. "Mrs. Brooks said I'd find you here," he said quietly. He looked at Mandy, then at Ella, who was peering curiously at the old books. A soft, genuine smile touched his lips. "She looks happier."

"She just needed a story," Mandy said, her heart doing a familiar, chaotic flutter.

"I think we all do," he admitted. He took a small step closer into the cozy space, and the air grew thick with unspoken words. His gaze was so intense, so full of a raw, fragile hope, that Mandy felt her breath catch in her throat. He was close enough now that she could see the exhaustion and the gratitude warring in his eyes.

Their moment was shattered by the boisterous arrival of Tessa and Jonah, who burst into the library carrying a large, rolled-up poster. "There you are!" Jonah announced. "It's time to talk Regatta Eve."

They spread the poster out on a large table. "We're in charge of the kids' lantern parade," Tessa explained, "and we are officially recruiting you." She pointed at Mandy, then at Logan. "And you, because you owe this town a little bit of light."

Logan flinched slightly, but he looked at Ella's excited face and nodded. "Okay," he said quietly. "We're in."

As the four of them began to brainstorm ideas, laughing at one of Jonah's terrible puns, Mandy glanced out the library window. Just for a moment, she saw a familiar, mud-splattered truck drive slowly past. It didn't stop, but she saw the silhouette of the driver. Caleb. A chill ran down her spine, a cold reminder that the fight in the diner wasn't over. It was just waiting for the next storm.

Shaking off the feeling, her eyes fell back on a box of donated books. A very old, leather-bound volume with no title was sitting on top. Curious, she picked it up. As she opened the cover, a folded, yellowed piece of paper slipped out. It was a letter, the handwriting an elegant, looping script.

"To my dearest L," it began. "If you are reading this, then the tide has brought my secret back to shore. Do not let them find the locket. It holds the truth of what happened that summer..."

The phrase "that summer" snagged in her mind, sharp as a fishhook. For a split second, the scent of old paper was replaced by the smell of salt and bonfire smoke, and she heard a faint, panicked cry that seemed to echo from her own memory. She shook her head, forcing the feeling away, focusing on the elegant, faded script in front of her. This wasn't a story about a grumpy badger. This was a real story, a secret held within the library walls, waiting to be discovered.

Chapter 9: Driftwood Promises

The community workday was Jonah's brilliant idea. On Saturday morning, half the town seemed to show up at the beach with hammers and a stubborn sense of civic pride. Mandy arrived feeling a familiar knot of anxiety, but it loosened when Tessa immediately handed her a pair of work gloves.

Then Jonah, in his self-appointed role as foreman, reassigned her. "Kline!" he called out. "Logan needs a hand holding the new rail steady while he secures it. You're up."

Mandy's heart did a nervous flip. She walked hesitantly toward the pier where Logan was working, intensely aware of him as a physical presence. "Jonah's orders," she said, trying to sound casual.

A small smile touched Logan's lips. "He thinks he's in charge." He positioned a long, smooth plank of new wood. "Just need you to hold it flush right here. Press hard."

Mandy gripped the plank. Logan moved closer, his shoulder brushing against hers as he lined up the drill. The high-pitched whir of the drill vibrated through the wood and up her arms, a powerful, buzzing current that seemed to connect them.

"Okay, lunch break," Jonah yelled from the shore.

Mandy was about to head back to Tessa when Logan stopped her. "Wait," he said, pulling a sandwich from a cooler. "My mom packed extra." He handed her the sandwich—turkey and swiss, her favorite.

"How did you know?" she asked, surprised.

"I remember things," he said with a small shrug.

They sat on the edge of the pier, eating in a comfortable silence. As they talked, Mandy got a prickling sensation on her neck, the unmistakable feeling of being watched. She scanned the crowd on the beach and saw her. Becca, the blonde from the boardwalk, was staring at them, her arms crossed. It wasn't a look of curiosity, but one of cold, hard judgment. Becca held her gaze for a moment before smirking and turning away.

Shaking off the unease, Mandy turned back to Logan. "The letter," she said suddenly. "The one I found in the book. It mentioned a locket."

Logan went still. "A locket?"

"It said it holds the truth of what happened 'that summer.' I feel like I should try to find it."

"My grandmother used to tell stories about a locket like that," he said, his voice dropping. "An old town tragedy. She said it was a story that broke a lot of hearts." He looked at her, his expression serious. "Be careful, Mandy. Digging up old ghosts can get you hurt."

Before she could ask what he meant, another voice, sharp and bitter, cut through their peace. "Playing hero again, Reyes?"

Caleb was standing a few feet away, a sneer on his face. "First a rescue, now you're rebuilding the whole town. What's next? Walking on water?"

Logan's body tensed. "Leave it alone, Caleb."

"I can't," Caleb said, his voice dropping, becoming more wounded than angry. "My dad and I built this section of rail with your brother. Michael loved this spot." He looked at Logan, his eyes filled with a raw, accusing pain. "And now you're just tearing it down like it was nothing."

The accusation hung in the air, heavy and cruel. "That's not what I'm doing," Logan said, his voice strained.

"Isn't it?" Caleb shot back. He started to stalk away, then stopped and glanced back. But he wasn't looking at Logan. His eyes, cold and intense, locked onto Mandy for a split second, as if to say, *You're part of this now*. Then he was gone, leaving Logan shrouded in grief and Mandy with a fresh spike of fear.

The rest of the afternoon was strained. As the workday wound down, Mandy started the walk back to her car, her mind reeling. As she approached it, she saw a small white envelope tucked under the windshield wiper.

Her name, *Mandy*, was written on the front in sharp, blocky letters.

Her hands trembling, she pulled it free and opened it. Inside was a single sheet of paper. There were no pleasantries, no signature. Just one typed, chilling line.

I know you remember more than you're letting on. Stop digging.

Chapter 10: Bonfire Confessions

The typed note felt like a brand on her mind. For two days, Mandy lived in a state of low-grade, humming terror. The words, *Stop digging*, echoed in her head. She clutched the secret to her chest, another heavy stone added to the weight she was already carrying.

When Tessa texted about a bonfire, Mandy's immediate response was a visceral *no*. But Tessa, relentless, showed up at her door. "You're coming," she said simply. "You can't let the ghosts win."

The bonfire that night was different. The circle was smaller, tighter—just the four of them. The air wasn't charged with awkwardness, but with a quiet, shared history forged in the heart of a storm. They sat around the crackling flames, listening to Jonah's clumsy but heartfelt guitar chords.

"I'm thinking of changing my major," Mandy heard herself say. "I went to college to study literature because I love stories, but I spent the whole year terrified of being asked for my own opinion. I made myself invisible." She looked at Logan, whose intense gaze made her feel both terrified and brave. "I don't want to be invisible anymore."

The confession hung in the air, simple and profound.

"You were never invisible to us," Tessa said, squeezing her hand.

After a moment, Logan spoke, his voice low and rough. "After the accident," he began, his eyes fixed on the dancing flames, "the one thing I wanted to do was surf. But I couldn't. It felt like... like I didn't deserve it. Like feeling that joy would be a betrayal of my brother." He finally looked up, his gaze finding Mandy's. "I dream about it. But I feel like I'm anchored to the bottom of the ocean."

His vulnerability was a raw, open wound, an echo of her own.

Eventually, Tessa and Jonah, with a shared, knowing glance, stood up. "We're going to search for the perfect marshmallow-roasting sticks," Jonah announced. "A sacred quest. We could be gone for a while."

They disappeared into the darkness, leaving Mandy and Logan alone. The air was suddenly thick with unspoken things.

"Thank you," Logan said softly, "for what you said. About not wanting to be invisible."

"Thank you for what you said," she replied, her voice barely a whisper. "About the ocean."

He moved closer. "I don't think you're invisible, Mandy," he said, his voice husky. "When I look at you, I feel like I'm seeing the only real thing on this whole beach."

He reached out, his fingers gently tucking a stray curl behind her ear. Just as he leaned in, a sharp *snap* of a twig echoed from the darkness of the dunes behind them. Mandy's head jerked toward the sound, her heart seizing. She saw nothing but shifting shadows, but the feeling of being watched was suddenly, terrifyingly real.

Logan didn't seem to notice. He leaned in slowly, his gaze searching hers, and then he kissed her.

It was hesitant, searching, and deeply, achingly real. It was the taste of salt and smoke and a year's worth of unspoken longing. For a heartbeat, she let herself melt into it. But then, the reality of it all—the note, the sound in the dunes, the feeling of being watched—crashed back in.

With a small, choked gasp, she pulled back. Logan's eyes were wide with confusion and hurt.

"I can't," she whispered, the words tearing from her throat.

"Is it me?" he asked, his voice cracking, so quiet she barely heard it. "Am I... too broken?"

The question was a knife to her heart. Before she could answer, before she could see the full extent of the damage she had just inflicted, she scrambled to her feet and fled. She ran from the boy, from the fire, from the beautiful, terrifying promise of a feeling she knew she didn't deserve. How could she let someone see her, truly see her, when she was still a ghost? How could she accept his light when she was so full of her own darkness and secrets? She ran into the cold, dark night, leaving him alone in the dying light of the bonfire.

Chapter 11: Underneath the Undertow

Mandy ran until her lungs burned, collapsing onto the cold, damp sand of the rocky cove. Logan's question echoed in the hollow space inside her, a shard of glass twisting in her heart. *Is it me? Am I... too broken?* She had taken his fragile, tentative step toward the light and crushed it. The shame was a physical weight, pressing down on her.

She spent the next day in a self-imposed exile. When she finally emerged, it was to escape the suffocating silence of the house. As she walked toward the shore, she saw him. Logan was standing at the end of the docks, alone, just staring blankly at the water. Even from a distance, she could see the hollowness in his posture, the way the light seemed to pass right through him. He looked like a ghost, and she was the one who had sent him there. The sight was a fresh stab of guilt, and she quickly turned away before he could see her.

She ended up at her cove, clutching the anonymous note. *Stop digging.* The threat felt inextricably linked to her flight from Logan. How could she pull him into her own dark undertow?

"The sea is a good listener," a familiar voice said. Mrs. Brooks was standing a few feet away. She sat on the boulder next to Mandy. "Fear is a powerful current, my dear. It will convince you that the safest thing to do is to let go of the boat and sink."

"What if you're the storm?" Mandy whispered. "What if you're the thing that's going to wreck the boat?"

"I once loved a man who was a sailor," Mrs. Brooks said, her voice soft with memory. "I was terrified of the sea, so I let my fear choose for me. He sailed away, and I stayed here, safe and sound." She turned to Mandy, her eyes filled with a deep, ancient wisdom. "And I have regretted it every single day for fifty years. Courage isn't the absence of fear, Mandy. It's holding on to the boat, even when you're terrified of the storm. And sometimes," she added, her gaze sharpening with intent, "the boat isn't a person.

Sometimes it's a place. A belief. The part of yourself you're most afraid to fight for."

The story settled over Mandy, a painful, poignant lesson. She resolved to let Logan be his own boat. She would pour everything she had into the reading program, building a wall of books around herself so high that no one could get in.

She was in the secret room, sorting books with a frantic energy, when Tessa found her. "I saw Logan this morning," Tessa said, confirming the hollowed-out look Mandy had already witnessed. "He's completely shut down again."

"I'm doing what's best for him," Mandy said, more to convince herself than Tessa. "I'm staying away."

Just as she said the words, she heard a commotion from the main library. She and Tessa walked out to see a man in a suit tacking a notice to the community bulletin board. A small crowd had gathered. In the midst of it, Mandy saw a familiar, unpleasant face: Mr. Harrison, the father of Becca, one of her chief tormentors in high school. He was a town councilman, and he was watching the proceedings with a look of grim satisfaction.

A chill went down Mandy's spine. She moved closer to read the notice. It was an announcement for an emergency town budget meeting. Due to a municipal shortfall, several "non-essential" community programs were being proposed for immediate defunding.

At the very top of the list, underlined in red ink, were the words: *Salt Haven Library Children's Reading Program.*

Mandy stared at the notice, the blood draining from her face. The one safe harbor she had chosen, the one boat she was supposed to fight for, was about to be sunk. And she had the sickening feeling that it was no accident.

Chapter 12: Drowned Words

The notice about the budget cut acted like a lit match tossed into the dry kindling of town gossip. Fueled by a desperate sense of purpose, Mandy tried to fight back. She spent a morning at the town hall, but her arguments were met with polite dismissal.

"It's a simple matter of fiscal responsibility, Ms. Kline," the junior councilwoman said, her tone final. "We have roads to pave."

As Mandy left the office, her heart heavy with defeat, she saw the councilwoman cross the lobby to join Mr. Harrison. They shared a laugh, and Mr. Harrison glanced over at Mandy with a cold, triumphant smile. It was a personal attack, a clear message that the system was rigged against her.

Feeling smaller and more invisible than ever, she was halfway to the exit when an older woman she didn't know gently touched her arm. The woman pressed a folded twenty-dollar bill into her hand. "For the reading program," she whispered, her eyes kind. "Some of us remember what matters. Don't give up." The unexpected gesture of support was a small, flickering light in a growing darkness.

Meanwhile, Logan heard the news from Jonah and retreated further into his grief. The thought that Mandy was moving on, building walls, was a cold weight in his chest. He showed up to pick Ella up from the library, his silence a fortress. One afternoon, he started to turn back, to say something—anything—to bridge the gap between them. But he saw Mandy across the room, completely absorbed in her work, her back to him. He mistook her focus for a deliberate snub, and the fragile impulse to connect died. The misunderstanding hardened his resolve to stay away.

Caleb found him at the docks later, staring out at the flat, calm sea. "Heard your girlfriend is trying to play town hero," Caleb said.

Logan didn't even look at him. "She's not my girlfriend."

"Good," Caleb said, his expression uncharacteristically serious. "Because you don't need that kind of trouble. The Harrisons have it out for her. You need to stay away from her, Logan. For your own good." The warning, though wrapped in cruelty, felt disturbingly like genuine concern, cementing Logan's belief that Mandy was a storm he needed to avoid.

The distance between them grew, a silent, painful thing their friends were powerless to bridge. The weight of it all became too much for Mandy. One evening, sitting alone in the secret room, she finally admitted defeat. She was a lightning rod for trouble. The whispers, the notes, Mr. Harrison's smug satisfaction, Logan's cold distance—she was the common denominator.

Her decision, when it came, was a quiet, heartbreaking surrender. She would see the regatta festivities through. She had made a promise to Ella. But after that, she would leave. She would pack her bags, go back to her empty dorm room, and disappear for good. It was the only way to protect them all from her ghosts. It was the only way to stop being the storm.

Chapter 13: Regatta Preparations

The week leading up to the regatta was a flurry of activity. For Mandy, it was a painful charade. She moved through the preparations like a ghost, her decision to leave a cold, hard stone in her gut. She had promised Ella she would help with the lantern parade, and she wouldn't break that promise.

The "committee"—Mandy, Logan, Tessa, and Jonah—gathered at a long picnic table near the docks, surrounded by a chaotic swarm of children. The air between Mandy and Logan was thick with a painful, polite tension.

"Why are you two sad?" Ella asked, her voice carrying in the bustling noise. "You don't talk anymore."

The innocent question was a gut punch to them both. "We're just busy, kiddo," Logan mumbled.

Mandy, needing to escape, moved to help a small boy who was struggling. As she leaned over, her bag tipped over, and her journal slid out, falling open on the bench.

Logan glanced over. He saw a page covered in a frantic, slanted script. A single, stark line wasn't crossed out: *A mouth full of sea glass, a heart full of ghosts.* It was raw, personal, and full of a pain that was clearly ancient. A wave of shame, cold and sharp, washed over him. He had been so wrapped up in his own grief, his own story, that he'd been blind to hers. He hadn't just been a wave; he'd been a selfish one, demanding she navigate his storm without ever asking about the sea she was already drowning in.

"Mandy."

She turned. Logan was looking at her, truly looking at her, for the first time in weeks. The cold distance in his eyes was gone, replaced by a look of profound, dawning regret.

Before he could say anything, Jonah appeared at her elbow, his expression grim. "Can I talk to you for a second?" he asked, his voice low.

He led her away from the noisy picnic table. "I found something out," Jonah said, refusing to meet her eyes.

"What is it, Jonah? You're scaring me."

"You're not going to like it, Mandy. Maybe it's better if I just handle it."

"Handle what?" she insisted. "Tell me."

He finally looked at her, his face tight with anger. "The note," he said. "The one on your car. It was Caleb."

The name hit her like a physical blow, but underneath the shock was a deeper, colder dread. Her mind flashed to the other note, the one from senior year. *He knows. He saw everything.* The blocky, anonymous letters on her windshield suddenly felt terrifyingly familiar. Could it have been him all along?

Chapter 14: Silent Waters

Jonah's words hung in the air, a poison dart that found its mark. *It was Caleb.* The world seemed to tilt on its axis, the cheerful sounds of the lantern-making fading into a dull, distant roar.

A cold, hard resolve began to form in the pit of her stomach. This was a quiet, steely anger. She was done being a ghost. She was done being scared.

"I have to talk to him," she said, her voice low and steady.

"Whoa, Mandy, I don't think that's a good idea," Jonah said. "Let me handle it."

"No," she said, her gaze unwavering. "I have to do this. Me."

She walked down the long stretch of the docks, the wooden planks thudding beneath her feet like a war drum. Caleb turned as she approached, his expression curdling when he saw her face.

"What do you want?" he asked.

She stopped a few feet from him, her body trembling, but she held his gaze. "The note," she said, her voice shaking but clear. "On my car. It was you."

Caleb's face went through a rapid series of emotions. "I don't know what you're talking about."

"Stop lying," Mandy said, taking another step closer. "Why, Caleb? Why would you do that?"

"You don't get it, do you?" he sneered. "You just show up here with your sad little story, and everyone just falls all over themselves to protect you. Even Logan. He was finally starting to forget, and then you came back. You and all your broken pieces."

"This has nothing to do with Logan," she shot back. "This is about you. You're a coward."

"I'm trying to save him!" he laughed, a bitter, ugly sound. "He needs to forget what happened. All of it."

"And what about what *you* did?" The question flew out of her. "You were there that night, weren't you? The night of the bonfire, senior year. You saw what happened."

The color drained from Caleb's face. "I... I don't..."

"You saw them push me," she whispered, the memory suddenly sharpening into a painful, horrifying clarity. *The bonfire's heat on her back, Becca's mocking laughter, the hard shove from behind, and Caleb's face in the crowd, illuminated by the flames, his expression frozen in shock before he turned away.* "You saw everything, and you did nothing. You just watched."

A collective gasp went through the small crowd of onlookers. Mandy's eyes flickered to Becca, who had gone pale, her smug expression replaced by one of pure panic as she quickly looked away, refusing to meet Mandy's gaze.

Before Caleb could respond, Logan's voice cut through the tension. "What's going on here?" He was walking toward them, his face a thundercloud.

"Stay out of this, Logan," Caleb snapped.

"No," Logan said, his voice dangerously calm.

But before he could take another step, Mandy held up a hand. "No, Logan," she said, her voice ringing with a newfound authority that stopped him in his tracks. "Please. This is mine."

Logan froze, stunned by the authority in her voice. This wasn't the fragile, quiet girl from the library. This was someone else, someone fierce and strong. A wave of awe, quickly followed by a pang of deep respect, washed over him. He had wanted to be her protector, but he realized in that moment that she didn't need one. She was her own hero.

She turned back to Caleb, her fear now completely burned away by a clean, righteous anger. "You've been hiding behind Logan's tragedy for a year, using it as an excuse to be cruel. But you have your own ghosts, don't you, Caleb? You're just as haunted as he is."

Just then, Ella ran up and tugged on Logan's hand. "Why is everyone yelling?"

Seeing his little sister seemed to break something in Caleb. The anger and bravado crumbled, leaving behind a raw, exposed shame. Without another word, he turned and fled.

The onlookers were whispering, staring. But for the first time, Mandy didn't feel the sting of their judgment. She just felt a quiet, trembling sense of vindication. She had faced the monster, and he had been the one to run.

As the crowd began to disperse, a low rumble echoed from far out at sea. Dark, heavy clouds were gathering on the horizon, a chilling echo of the night that had changed everything, a promise that the storm was not yet over.

Chapter 15: Nighttime Rescue Redux

The storm didn't wait. The low rumble became a deafening crack of thunder, and the cheerful festival grounds dissolved into chaos as rain fell in a solid, blinding sheet.

In the confusion, Mandy lost sight of Logan and Ella. She finally broke free from the panicked crowd and saw him standing near the edge of the harbor, spinning in a slow, desperate circle. "Ella!" he was screaming, his voice raw with a panic that was terrifyingly familiar. "She's gone!"

Mandy's blood ran cold. This was a horrifying echo of the first rescue, but infinitely worse. This was Ella. Her mind raced. She remembered Ella talking about a small, hidden cove with smooth, gray stones she called "mermaid's tears."

"Logan!" Mandy shouted, grabbing his arm. "The cove! Past the rocks! She might have gone there!"

He understood immediately. They ran, their feet slipping on the wet sand. As they rounded the rocky outcrop, their worst fears were realized. The tide was high, the waves crashing violently. And inside, huddled on a small ledge that was rapidly disappearing, was a small, terrified figure.

"ELLA!" Logan screamed, his voice breaking. He started to run forward, but then he froze, his body rigid, his eyes locked on the violent water. Mandy saw the memory take hold, the ghost of his brother rising from the waves to paralyze him.

"Logan?" she said, her voice shaking. He didn't respond. He was trapped, drowning on dry land.

In that moment, something inside Mandy shifted. A fierce, protective resolve burned hotter than her fear. "Stay here! Call for help!" she yelled at Logan, her voice ringing with authority. She scrambled over the slippery rocks, finding a higher path.

"Mandy!" Ella cried over the roar of the ocean.

"I'm coming, Ella! Just hold on!" Mandy shouted back, finally reaching the ledge. The water was already swirling around their ankles. "I'm scared," Ella sobbed, clinging to her.

"I know. But we're going to be brave together," Mandy said, her arm a tight, protective circle around the shivering child.

Her voice seemed to break the spell that held Logan captive. He snapped back to reality, his eyes focusing on Mandy protecting his sister. He saw her courage, and it became his own. He plunged into the water, fighting his way toward them. For a brief second, his eyes met Mandy's over Ella's head. In that single, silent look, she saw everything: his shame, his terror, and a profound, desperate gratitude. She held his gaze, her own eyes promising that she wouldn't let go.

"I've got you!" he yelled. "Both of you!"

Together, they navigated the treacherous path back, finally collapsing onto the main beach in a heap of soaked, shivering relief. Logan didn't just hug his sister; he instinctively reached for Mandy, pulling her into the desperate embrace, needing to feel them both safe. His body was wracked with sobs of gratitude, terror, and a profound, shattering shame.

The rain began to soften. He finally looked up at her, his face a raw canvas of emotion. He framed her face with his hands, his thumbs wiping the rain and tears from her cheeks. "You saved her," he whispered. "I... I froze."

"It's okay to be scared, Logan," she said softly.

"No, you don't understand," he said, his voice thick with a truth that had been buried for a year. "I love you."

The words hung in the air, a raw, desperate admission, a drowning man naming his lighthouse. Tears streamed down Mandy's face. All the walls she had built, all the reasons she had to run, crumbled to dust. "I love you, too," she confessed.

He leaned in and kissed her, and this time, there was no hesitation. It was a kiss of desperation and relief, of gratitude and a fierce, terrifying hope. He broke away for a second, his forehead resting against hers.

"Don't leave," he whispered, his voice pleading. "Please. Stay."

The kiss wasn't just about the storm they had survived; it was a promise to face the ones still coming. Together.

Chapter 16: High Tide

The world after the storm was unnaturally quiet. Logan drove them to his house, the three of them wrapped in blankets. The Reyes's porch light cast a warm, welcoming glow in the misty, post-rain darkness.

As they walked through the front door, Logan's parents rushed to meet them, their faces a mixture of terror and profound relief. His mother pulled Ella into a fierce hug before turning to Logan. His father, a quiet, stoic man, simply put a hand on Logan's shoulder, a gesture that conveyed a universe of unspoken emotion. Their eyes fell on Mandy, and there was only a deep, quiet gratitude. "Thank you," Logan's mom whispered, her voice thick with tears.

They ushered Ella upstairs, leaving Logan and Mandy alone. He sank onto the sofa, and she sat beside him, their hands finding each other instinctively. "I need to tell them," he said, his voice low and resolute. "Everything."

When his parents came back downstairs, Logan didn't let go of Mandy's hand. Her presence was his anchor. "I'm sorry," he began, his voice cracking. "I'm sorry I shut you out. I thought I had to be strong for you."

"Oh, Logan," his mother breathed. "We never wanted you to be strong. We just wanted our son."

"The day Michael died," Logan said, the confession finally spilling out. "It wasn't just a freak wave. We were daring each other. It was my idea. I challenged him." He squeezed his eyes shut. "He got caught in the rip current. I tried to pull him out, but I wasn't strong enough. He slipped... his hand just slipped right out of mine."

He finally broke. His father moved to the sofa and wrapped his arms around his son. "I'm sorry, son," his father whispered, his own voice thick with emotion. "I was so lost in my own grief, I forgot that you were lost, too. I should have talked to you." For the first time since the accident, the three of them grieved together.

As Mandy watched them, a family finally beginning to mend, she felt something shift inside her. She had spent so long feeling like a ghost, defined by a secret she couldn't face. But seeing Logan speak his truth, seeing the love that met him on the other side, she realized that secrets only have power when you keep them in the dark. For the first time, the thought of facing her own past didn't feel like a terrifying end, but a possible beginning.

Later, Mandy found him on the back porch. "You did a brave thing in there," she said softly.

"It didn't feel brave," he said, turning to her. "It just felt... necessary." He looked at her, his eyes clear for the first time in a year. "I spent so long trying to outrun that memory. But you can't outrun the ocean. You have to learn to swim in it." He gently pulled her closer. "You taught me that."

Ella appeared on the porch in her pajamas and wrapped her small arms around Mandy's legs. "You were brave, Mandy," she whispered. "You were my hero."

Mandy's heart swelled. She knelt and hugged the little girl back. "We were brave together."

When Ella had gone back to bed, Logan looked at Mandy, a small, hopeful smile on his face. "My dad used to say that forgiveness is like the high tide. It comes in slowly, but it washes the whole beach clean." He paused, his expression growing serious. "It doesn't mean the storms won't come back. But it means we'll be ready for them."

He leaned down and kissed her, a gentle, promising kiss that was worlds away from the desperate one on the beach. It wasn't a kiss born of a storm, but of the quiet, hopeful calm that follows. It was the feeling of the tide turning, a promise to be each other's anchor in the fights still to come.

Chapter 17: Low Tide Letters

The day after the storm, Mandy found herself drawn to the library's secret room. Bolstered by a new courage, she'd asked her mom to bring down a dusty box from the attic. Inside, she found a sealed envelope with the words "To My Future Friend" written on the front.

Dear Friend, it began. *I hope you like books as much as I do. I hope you're not afraid of the ocean, even when it's angry. I hope you're brave and kind, and that you know how to make people feel seen, even when they feel invisible. I'll be waiting for you in Salt Haven.*

Tears welled in Mandy's eyes. It was a perfect, heartbreaking portrait of the connection she had craved her entire life.

"Find something interesting?" Logan's voice was soft from the doorway. He sat beside her and read the letter she handed him.

"It sounds like she was waiting for you," he said, his voice thick.

"I think she was," Mandy whispered.

He took her hand. "Mandy," he said, his voice serious. "I want to be that friend. I want to face whatever comes next—the library, Caleb, your past—all of it. Together. If you'll let me."

His words were a balm, but a cold knot of fear remained. Facing Caleb was one thing. Facing the full memory of that night, the memory she had buried so deep, was another. Could she really share that darkness with him? Still, she looked at him, at his earnest, hopeful face, and knew she had to try. "Yes," she said, her heart full. "Together."

He leaned in and kissed her, a slow, tender kiss that was a quiet affirmation of their new beginning.

The moment was interrupted by a soft knock. Mrs. Brooks stood in the doorway. "I don't mean to interrupt," she said with a twinkle in her eye. "I just thought this might be a good time for a riddle. What is a treasure that is lighter the more of it you share?"

"A story," Mandy and Logan said in unison.

"Precisely," Mrs. Brooks said. She placed a very old, beautiful book on the table between them. "Every story deserves to be told." With a final, knowing smile, she left them alone.

Curious, Mandy opened the book. Tucked inside was not a letter, but a faded black-and-white photograph of a young woman standing on the Salt Haven pier. She had a defiant smile and, gleaming against her dress, was a distinctive, heart-shaped locket.

Before they could process the new clue, Tessa and Jonah burst into the room, their faces alight with triumphant energy.

"You are not going to believe this!" Tessa said.

"The town council held an emergency press conference," Jonah continued. "After the story of the rescue got out—your story—public opinion shifted. Hard."

"Mr. Harrison was practically shamed into reversing his position," Tessa added. "And that's not even the best part. An anonymous donor has stepped forward to match any funds the community raises for the library. The reading program is safe, Mandy. You saved it."

The news hit Mandy with the force of a joyful, cleansing wave. Surrounded by her friends, her hand held securely in Logan's, she felt the last of her own walls crumble away.

Miles away, in his quiet house, Caleb Munroe hung up the phone with his father's financial advisor.

"Yes, that's right," he said, his voice low and strained. "The donation is to be made anonymously. No one needs to know where it came from."

He ended the call and stared out the window, his reflection a pale, haunted ghost in the glass. It didn't fix anything. It didn't erase the notes, or the things he'd said, or the things he'd failed to do. But it was a start. It was the first stone he'd ever tried to place back on the wall, instead of tearing it down.

Chapter 18: Regatta Eve

Regatta Eve descended on Salt Haven in a wave of twinkling lights and joyful noise. The harbor was alive, the air thick with the smell of fried dough, salty sea spray, and the excited chatter of a town ready to celebrate.

For the first time since her return, Mandy felt a part of it all. As dusk settled, she led the children's lantern parade along the boardwalk, a small, glowing river of light and laughter. As they passed the main stage, she saw Becca standing with a group of friends. Their eyes met, and instead of the usual smirk, Becca looked deeply uncomfortable, her face flushing with shame before she quickly looked away, unable to hold Mandy's gaze. It was a small, silent surrender, but for Mandy, it felt like a final, quiet victory.

After the parade, Logan took her hand and led her away from the noisy crowd, toward a quiet stretch of beach. They sat on the cool sand, the gentle waves lapping at the shore.

"I never thought I'd feel this way again," Logan said, his voice quiet. "Like I was a part of this town."

"Me neither," Mandy admitted.

He pulled the old, faded photograph from his pocket, the one of the defiant young woman with the heart-shaped locket. "What do you think her story is?" he asked.

"I don't know," Mandy said, tracing the image. "But I think Mrs. Brooks wants us to find out."

"Wait," Logan said, leaning closer and pointing at the photo. "Look behind her. Is that the old lighthouse keeper's cottage? The one that burned down fifty years ago?" It was. The clue gave their quest a new, tangible direction.

From their vantage point, Mandy spotted Caleb standing alone near the edge of the crowd, looking lost. He caught her eye for a moment before quickly looking away.

"Jonah told me about the donation," Logan said, following her gaze. "And Tessa saw him earlier. He asked her to tell you... he was sorry. For everything."

"I don't know what to think about it," Mandy confessed. "It doesn't erase what he did."

"No, it doesn't," Logan agreed. "But maybe... maybe it's his way of trying to find his way back. Maybe everyone deserves a chance to rewrite their story." He turned to her, his expression serious and full of a gentle, patient love. "Including you."

He took her hand. "You don't have to tell me," he said softly. "Not until you're ready. But when you are, I want to know everything. Not because I want to fix it, but because I want to help you carry it. I want to know your whole story, Mandy. The beauty and the terror."

His words were the key she had been waiting for. "Soon," she promised, her voice thick with emotion. "I'll tell you soon."

He stood up and pulled her to her feet. "Come on," he said, a slow smile spreading across his face. "I think I owe you a dance."

He led her back toward the lights, to a small, cleared space on the docks where couples were swaying to a slow song. He pulled her into his arms, and they moved together, a silent, perfect rhythm. He wasn't the broken boy, and she wasn't the invisible girl. They were just two people, holding on to each other under the stars, their hearts finally, blessedly, in the same tide.

Chapter 19: After the Bonfire

The festival was winding down. Instead of going home, Logan led Mandy to the quiet, secluded cove where they'd shared their first bonfire confessions.

"Okay," Mandy said, her voice a soft whisper in the night. "I'm ready."

Logan simply took her hand, his touch a steady, grounding presence.

"Senior year," she began, her eyes fixed on the dark, endless sea. "There was a bonfire here... I tried to leave, but they cornered me. Becca snatched a poem from my bag." Her memory was sharp now, a clear, painful image. "I tried to get it back, and one of them pushed me. Hard. I fell backward, down that small embankment by the dunes.

I hit my head. The worst part wasn't the fall. It was the silence afterward. They just... left me there. And Caleb... he saw the whole thing. He saw me fall, and he saw them run. And he just turned his back."

Logan's grip on her hand tightened, his face a mask of quiet, protective fury.

"I wasn't seriously hurt," she said. "But the shame of it... of being so worthless that no one would even check on me... I buried it. I forced myself to forget."

When she finished, Logan simply pulled her into his arms, holding her tightly. "Thank you for trusting me with your story," he whispered into her hair. "You are not worthless, Mandy. You are the bravest person I know." In that moment, the last of her ghosts seemed to dissolve, banished by the simple, powerful light of his acceptance.

The next day, they walked to the ruins of the old lighthouse keeper's cottage. They found the locket almost immediately, tucked into a loose stone in the old hearth. Inside were two tiny, folded pieces of paper. One was a love letter. The other was a confession. The lighthouse keeper's daughter hadn't been waiting for a lost love. She had been running from a powerful, cruel man she was being forced to marry: a young Mr. Harrison.

"The Harrisons," Mandy breathed, the historical irony sending a chill down her spine. Her victory over the town council felt suddenly deeper, a historical correction.

As they were leaving the ruins, a figure stepped onto the path. It was Caleb. He looked pale and nervous, and he wouldn't meet their eyes.

"I..." he started, his voice rough. "I can't fix what I did. But I wanted you to have this." He held out a small, faded photograph. "It was from that night. Before. I don't know why I kept it. I'm sorry."

Mandy took the photo. It was of her, standing by the bonfire, laughing at something one of her friends had said. She looked happy, carefree, and whole. It was a picture of the girl she'd been before the fall. It was a tangible piece of the past he had helped ruin, and now, in his own broken way, he was trying to give it back.

They walked back to the cove, the site of so much pain, and stood at the water's edge. Logan pulled the smooth, gray stone from his pocket and placed it in Mandy's hand. "Let's make a new memory for this cove," he said softly.

Together, they drew their arms back and threw the stone as hard as they could. It skipped once, twice, and then disappeared into the vast, blue water, a symbolic release of old pain, a promise of a new story for this place.

"I'm going back to college," Mandy said, her voice full of a new, solid confidence. "And I'm going to change my major to creative writing. I'm going to help other people tell their stories."

"And I'm going to start training for the surf championships next spring," Logan said, a genuine, unburdened smile on his face. "I'll come visit you. We'll make it work."

It wasn't a promise of a perfect, easy future. They both knew that healing was a slow tide, not a sudden wave. But it was a promise to face the currents together, to be each other's anchor, to hold on tight, no matter how stormy the sea became.

Chapter 20: Whispers Beneath the Tides

The sun was just beginning to rise, painting the calm, quiet ocean in hues of soft pink and pale gold. It was a stark, beautiful contrast to the stormy evening that had welcomed Mandy home. She stood on the pier, the same pier where she had first seen Logan as a ghost, but this time, she wasn't alone. His hand was warm and steady in hers.

As they walked, an old fisherman setting out for the day tipped his hat to them. "Morning, you two," he called out, his voice raspy and kind. "Good to see the sun out." It was a simple, public acknowledgment of them as a couple, a quiet welcome back into the fold of the town.

"It's funny," Mandy said, her voice soft in the morning quiet. "I came back to Salt Haven hoping the town would heal me. But it wasn't the town. It was the people." She squeezed his hand. "It was you."

"I think we healed each other," Logan replied, his gaze fixed on the horizon. "For the first time in a year, the ocean... it sounds right again. It's not angry. It's not sad. It just... is." He turned to her, a slow, easy smile on his face. "It sounds like home."

They reached the end of the pier and found a small, wrapped package sitting on their favorite bench. Inside was a beautiful, blank leather-bound journal. Tucked into the first page was a note in Mrs. Brooks's elegant script: *Every story needs an epilogue. Go write yours.*

Mandy laughed, clutching the journal to her chest. They stood there, watching the light dance on the water, replaying the memories of the summer—a tapestry woven from both beauty and terror.

"I promise to send you a copy of the first story I write," Mandy said, leaning her head on his shoulder.

"And I'll send you a picture from the winner's podium," he teased gently. He pulled out his phone. "In fact, what weekend in October are you free? I'm booking my bus ticket now."

"It's a deal," she laughed, her heart full.

He pulled her into his arms, holding her close. It was a hug full of quiet confidence and a deep, abiding love. It held the promise of late-night phone calls, of weekend visits, of a future that was no longer an unwritten dream, but a plan already in motion.

The sun finally cleared the horizon, flooding the world with a warm, brilliant light. The whispers of the past, the ones that had haunted the tides of Salt Haven, were finally quiet. All that was left was the sound of the waves, the warmth of the sun, and the steady, hopeful beat of two hearts, finally in sync, ready for whatever came next.

Acknowledgements

Writing *Whispers Beneath the Tides* has been a journey of memory, emotion, and rediscovery—much like the story itself.

To my early readers and critique partners: thank you for your honest insights, your encouragement, and your belief in Mandy and Logan's story before it found its final form. Your feedback was the tide that carried this book forward.

To my friends and family: your patience, support, and understanding—especially during the long nights and quiet stretches—mean more than you know. You kept me grounded when I was lost in Driftwood Point.

And to you, the reader: thank you for taking a chance on this story. For every heart that still aches for a second chance or wonders what might have been—this book is for you.

With gratitude,

Trevor Jensen

About the Author

Trevor Jensen writes emotionally rich, character-driven stories that explore the quiet ache of lost love, the redemptive power of second chances, and the moments that shape who we become. With a passion for coastal settings, slow-burn romance, and imperfect people trying to make sense of their hearts, his novels invite readers to linger in the in-between—where love hurts, heals, and dares to begin again.

When he's not writing, Trevor can usually be found walking near the water, collecting old postcards, or haunting used bookstores in search of forgotten stories. He believes some places stay with you forever—and some stories only surface when you're finally ready to hear them.

Whispers Beneath the Tides is his latest novel.

To see more of Trevor Jensen's publications, please visit his coming-soon web site at:

http://www.TrevorJensenBooks.com

www.ingramcontent.com/pod-product-compliance
Lightning Source LLC
Chambersburg PA
CBHW031308120726
47906CB00003B/946